WHEN MOM D[...]OYS

Written by Angela René Tuckett

Illustrated by Anaís Balbás

When we think of deployments we think of America's finest...Air Force, Army,

Marines, Navy & Coast Guard going to unforeseen locations overseas for an

extended amount of time and sometimes a return from a deployment is not

favorable. Oftentimes we forget to think of the ramifications of those deployments

and the long term affects this must have on our children. I hope this will enable a

platform for discussion on the importance of the mental and phycological health

of children of the military where resiliency has become an expectation. This book

was designed to enhance the realization that children are not alone and the need

for this to be acknowledged is crucial in establishing mental stability. We are a

network with an abundance of resources and guidance at our fingertips....

utilization is pivotal!

2019 © Angela René Tuckett
All rights reserved
Editor Sue Vander Hook
Illustrator Anaís Balbás

ISBN:9781704236162

This book is dedicated to my children Gage, Kai, Ayden & Addison who weathered the seasons with me throughout my journey in the military. You are the anchor that has kept me grounded!

Today momma is taking us to the zoo. We spend lots of time together always doing something new.

I love to go to the park and dance from here to the moon!

Sometimes we just hang out in our pajamas and watch my favorite cartoon.

Momma always reads to me and kisses me goodnight! She makes me feel so safe until the next daylight!

My mom is in the military, which isn't all that strange.

Tomorrow she is leaving and a lot is going to change.

Today I get to wave my flag and kiss my mom goodbye. My momma hugged me tight and whispered "The time is going to fly."

Daddy said it's okay to feel sad inside my heart. It's hard for the entire family that we have to be apart.

But momma is fighting for our country and being strong for me, so I'll be tough and I'll be strong and I'll be all that I can be.

FALL

I have a jar with 250 golden stars in it. Everyday I take one out and on my calendar they fit!

When the stars are gone, the jar will be all empty. That means the day has come that I get to see my mommy.

My daddy helps me make my mom some very special cards.
I like to send her pictures of the American flag she guards!

Today is Halloween and I dressed up as batgirl. I wish my mom were here to see me do a twirl! I'm having so much fun - all my friends are here with me. My momma would be happy - a smile she would see!

Today my teacher picked me to do my show and share. I showed a picture of mommy and told them how much I care.

I am so excited! Today is finally the day!
My mommy's coming back. That's all that I could say.

My momma's finally home, and I'm hugging her so tight. We're all together again, and everything's just right!

MISSING YOU!

Made in the USA
Monee, IL
10 November 2020